A JUST ONE MORE BOOK
Just For You

Apple Tree! Apple Tree!

by Mary Blocksma

Illustrated by Sandra Cox Kalthoff

Developed by The Hampton-Brown Company, Inc.

CHILDRENS PRESS, CHICAGO

Word List

Give children books they can read by themselves, and they'll always ask for JUST ONE MORE. This book is written with 59 of the most basic words in our language, all repeated in an appealing rhythm and rhyme.

a	friend	little	some
all	fruit	look	stay
an			
and	gift	me	that
apple(s)	go	more	the
at	good	my	them
away	grow		then
		no	to
be	have	not	too
boy	here	now	toy
	house		tree
can		oh	
	I	one	what
did	is		who
do	it	see	will
		seed(s)	with
fall	just	sleep	worm
for		snow	
	know		yes
			you

Library of Congress Cataloging in Publication Data

Blocksma, Mary.
  Apple tree! Apple tree!

  (Just one more)
  SUMMARY: The apple tree is a friend to all but longs for a true friend of its own.
  [1. Trees—Fiction.   2. Friendship—Fiction.
3. Stories in rhyme]   I. Kalthoff, Sandra Cox, ill.
II. Title.
PZ8.3.B5983Ap   1983   [E]   82–19852
ISBN 0—516–01584–2

1 2 3 4 5 6 7 8 9 10 R 91 90 89 88 87 86 85 84 83

Look at me and you will see
what a friend a tree can be.

Apple tree!
Apple tree!
Do you have a gift for me?

Yes, I have some fruit for you.
I have some fruit,
and good fruit, too.
I have some apples just for you.

11

Apple tree!
Apple tree!
Do you have a worm for me?

No!   I have no worm for you.
Worm is my friend,
and a good friend, too.
An apple seed will have to do.

Oh no! I have to go.
See my apple.
It will fall.
Then I will have
no house at all.

Just ONE apple?
That is all.
Just one more,
and it will fall.

Now I have no house.
I have no toy.
I have no good gift
for a boy.

I have no fruit.
I have no seeds.
I have no good friend
just for me.

Look, Tree.
Here is the snow.
You have to sleep.
I have to go.

Sleep, Tree.
THEN you will see
a good friend
for an apple tree.

21

Now I have a friend to stay,
a friend who will not go away.
Now I have an apple tree
to be a good friend just for me . . .